Mona Lotta

Weedy

Dee Monic

Baby Warty

Claws II

Bella Donna

BASH BELLA DONNA

Miss Batting

Peggy Leg

Claws I

Scatty

Witch Hazel

Clawpatra

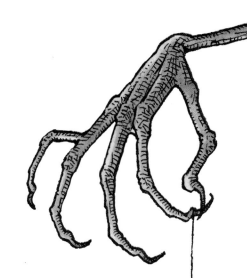

To three wicked witches -
Caroline, Suzie, and Rachel
A. C.

To my wife Lorna, for her
patience and inspiration
G. P.

First published in Great Britain by
Kingfisher Books, Grisewood & Dempsey, Ltd.

Text copyright © 1991 by Annie Civardi.
Illustrations copyright © 1991 by Graham Philpot.
All rights reserved. Published in the U.S.A. by Scholastic Inc.
730 Broadway, New York, NY 10003, by arrangement with
David Bennett Books, Ltd., 94 Victoria Street
St. Albans, Herts, AL1 3TG, England.
CARTWHEEL BOOKS is a trademark of Scholastic Inc.

Library of Congress Cataloging-in-Publication Data
Civardi, Annie.
    The wacky book of witches / written by Annie Civardi : illustrated
by Graham Philpot.
        p.   cm.
    "First published in Great Britain by Kingfisher Books, Grisewood &
Dempsey, Ltd."—T.p. verso.
    Summary: A compendium of witch rhymes, recipes, and spells.
    ISBN 0-590-45094-8
    1. Witchcraft—Literary collections.   2. Children's literature.
[1. Witches—Literary collections.]   I. Philpot, Graham, ill.
II. Title.
PZ5.C54   1991
818′.5467—dc20   91-43281
                                                             CIP
                                                             AC

Handlettering by Roger Hands

Produced and directed by
David Bennett Books, Ltd.

Typesetting by Type City
Production by Imago

ISBN 0-590-45094-8

12 11 10 9 8 7 6 5 4 3 2 1   2 3 4 5 6 7 /9

Printed in Mexico

First Scholastic printing, September 1992

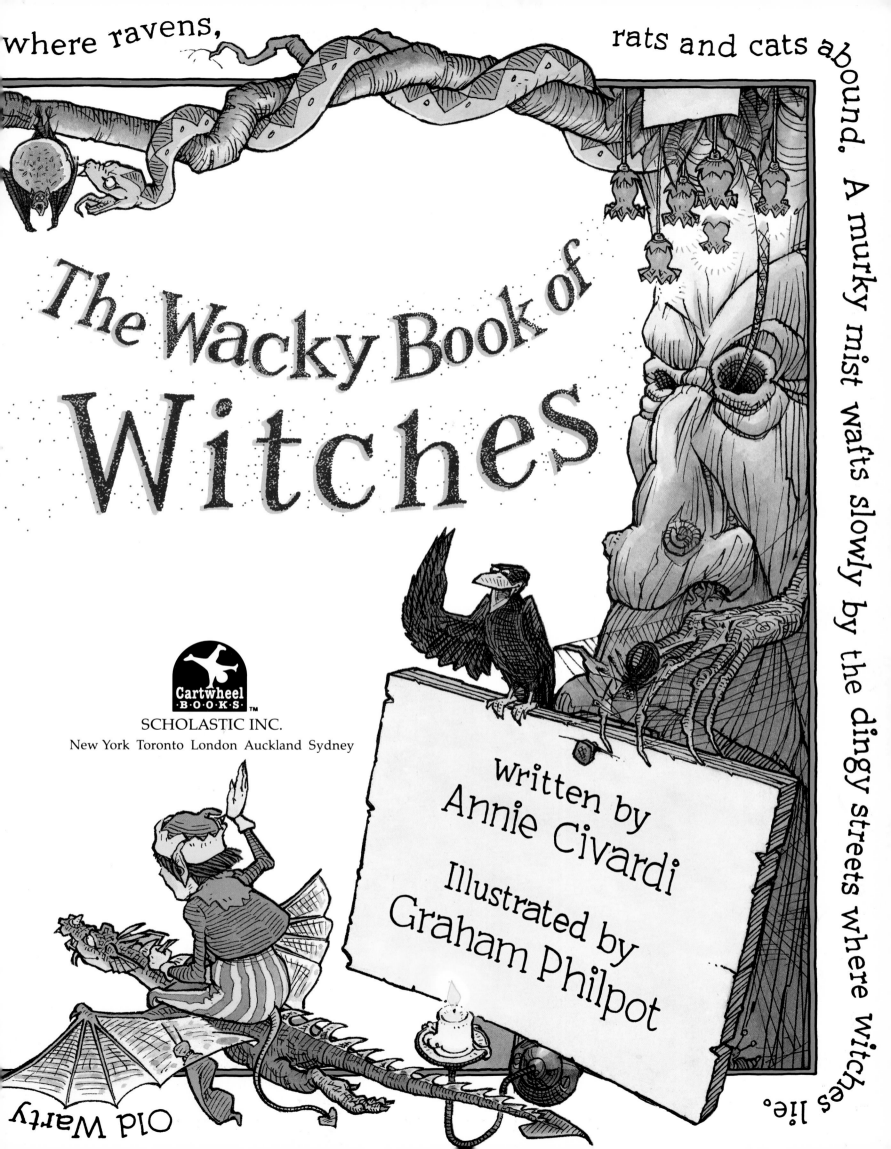

where ravens, rats and cats abound. A murky mist wafts slowly by the dingy streets where witches life.

The Wacky Book of Witches

Cartwheel
B·O·O·K·S ™
SCHOLASTIC INC.
New York Toronto London Auckland Sydney

Written by
Annie Civardi

Illustrated by
Graham Philpot

Old Warty

Welcome to
Cackle Town

In Cackle Town it's getting dark.
The sun has set
o'er Broomstick Park.
The moon is full, the stars are bright,
There's witchy work to do tonight.
The bells ring loud
from Warty's tower.
It's time to start the Witching Hour!

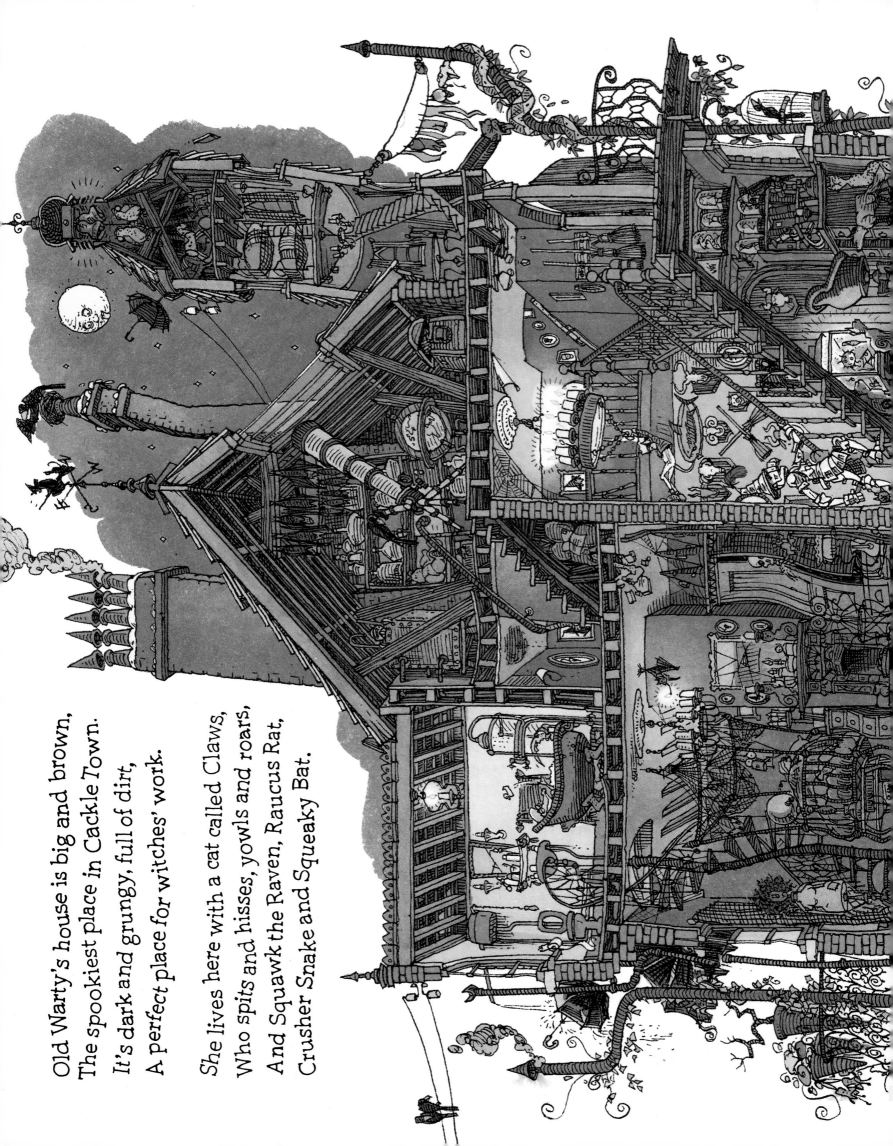

Old Warty's house is big and brown,
The spookiest place in Cackle Town.
It's dark and grungy, full of dirt,
A perfect place for witches' work.

She lives here with a cat called Claws,
Who spits and hisses, yowls and roars,
And Squawk the Raven, Raucus Rat,
Crusher Snake and Squeaky Bat.

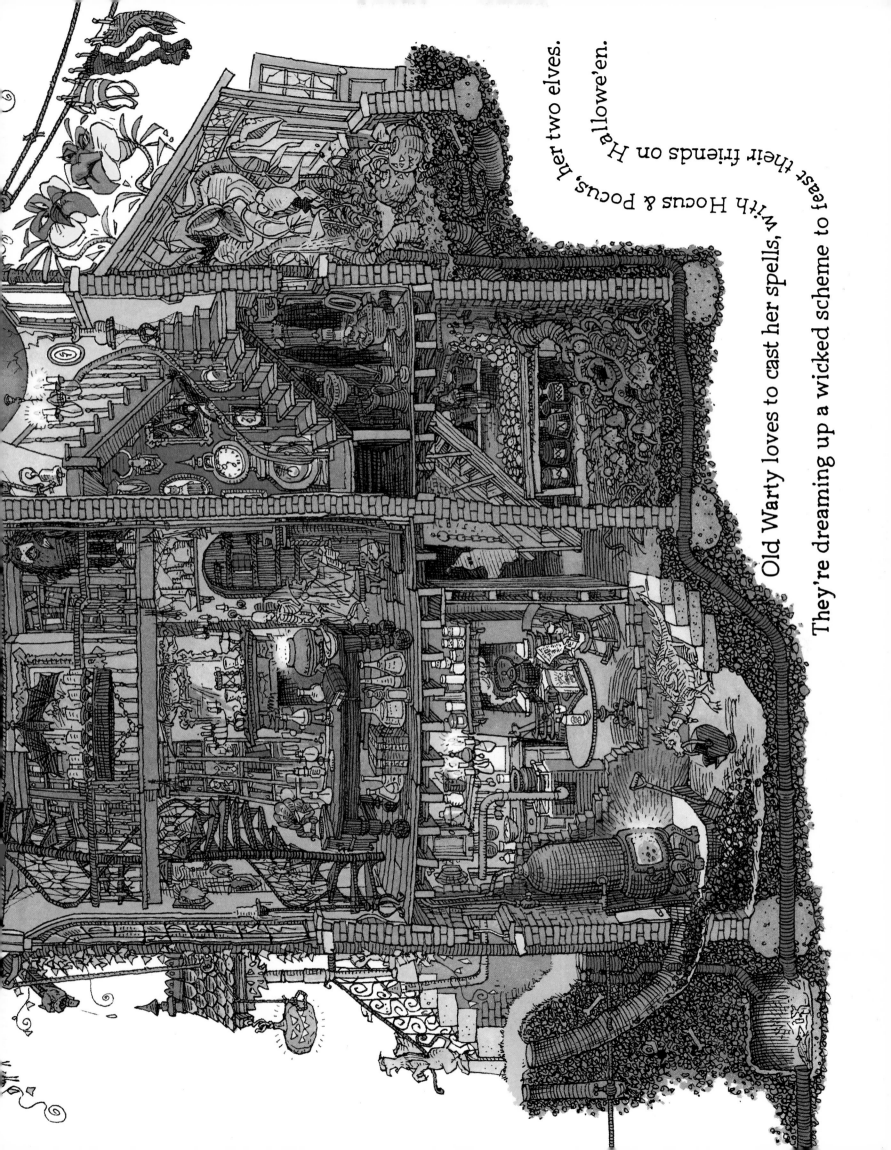

Old Warty loves to cast her spells, her two elves.

With Hocus & Pocus, her two elves.

They're dreaming up a wicked scheme to feast their friends on Hallowe'en.

At eight o'clock in Warty's room
Her ghostly clock begins to boom.
Asleep she looks a dreadful sight;
She's even worse when it gets light.
The only way to make her rise
Is bonk her head
and poke her eyes.

At last old Warty's out of bed.

She snorts and burps now she's been fed.

Her pets all help her bathe and dress.

They make her look a ghastly mess.

And now she's off to buy some meat

From Ratty's shop in old Screech Street.

Then on to Batty's for her wig. It's full of spiders foul and big. She buys a veil of spider's lace to hide her ugly, warty face.

She sells the ... And last she visits good old Peg, a witch who has a wooden leg.

To Grewsome Gardens witches go
Where pumpkins, beats and painsies grow.
Old Warty's come to work as well
To find things for her froggy spell.
She picks up worms and slimy slugs
And lots of other nasty bugs.
For stewing bones she digs down deep
Within the smelly compost heap.

A witch's work is never done,
So to the Charmless School
    they've come.
Before the moon begins to fade
They'll learn to spell and serenade.
Miss Spelling's lesson is the first –
She finds which witch can
    spell the worst.

of all the rest. She sweeps ahead she's the best.

Before old Warty makes a stew
There's one more thing she has to do.
She goes to Broomstick Park to meet
The wicked witches from her street.
They're showing off their spelling craft –
Not all are spooky; some are daft.
Bad Pocus Elf is there as well.
He's going to cast a grisly spell.

Turtle tongues
and hair of dog,
Turn Helen's cat
into a frog.

ZAP

POW

rivet
rivet

BOINGG

Hubble bubble, make this plant
Grow bigger than my Weedy aunt.

KER-RUMP

KER-RASH

Yur
Yur

Hel

Now Warty's feast is in full swing—
A party that's got everything.
There's ghastly games and witchy brew,
And Warty's special Pumpkin Stew.
In Cackle Town, they've never seen
A wilder time on Hallowe'en!